LAST CHANCE CHRISTMAS
A Fairfield Corners Novella

L.A. REMENICKY

Lavish
Publishing LLC

Contents

Chapter 1	1
Chapter 2	6
Chapter 3	12
Chapter 4	15
Chapter 5	20
Chapter 6	28
Chapter 7	35
Chapter 8	41
Chapter 9	48
Chapter 10	60
Also by L.A. Remenicky	67
About the Author	71
Also from the Lavish Publishing family	73

LAST CHANCE CHRISTMAS. Copyright 2016 ©

First Edition

2016 Lavish Publishing, LLC

All Rights Reserved

Published in the United States by Lavish Publishing, LLC, Midland, Texas

Cover Design by: Wyked Ink

Cover Images: Adobe Stock

Paperback Edition

ISBN: 9781944985226

www.LavishPublishing.com

Chapter One

IT WAS FINALLY OVER. His last case with the US Marshalls was closed, and he was officially released. His phone buzzed weakly on the seat where it lay forgotten as he drove north on Interstate 69 on his trip home from Louisiana. Burnt out from dealing with the underbelly of society, he was ready for a fresh start in the small Indiana town he now called home. The only thing missing was his Jojo. Unemployed, he now had time to win her back. At least that damn money was good for something; he could take his time and find a job that interested him.

When he pulled into the rest area on the north side of Indianapolis for a nap and a soda before finishing the last two hours of his journey, he discovered he had neglected to plug his phone into the car charger. Worry clawed at his stomach when he plugged in the charger, and notifications of missed calls and texts from his ex-partner, Jax McKenna, popped up on the screen. The messages were short and didn't go into detail, but there was an emergency with his pregnant wife. As he dialed Jax's cell phone number, he prayed under his breath that Lainie and the baby would be okay.

When he hung up the phone, he was still worried, just not about Lainie and the baby. Now he was worried about Jax's sister, Jordan, his Jojo. Jax had been trying to call her for over four hours with no contact. Jordan wouldn't ignore Jax's voice mails, especially since they were about Lainie and the baby.

The last time she was out of touch for that long, her asshole ex-husband, who had been physically and emotionally abusing Jordan the entire time they were married, had forbidden Jordan to talk to her brother. When Brent found out, he wanted to track down her ex and beat him to a bloody pulp for treating a woman that way, especially Jordan. He almost lost his job when he beat up a suspect after witnessing the jackass hitting his girlfriend. That was the day he finally admitted to himself that he wanted Jordan. It wasn't until Jax was on the run with Lainie that he finally had the chance to act on his feelings.

Hard to believe the legendary Brent Halston had fallen for the strong, resilient doctor. Jax had punched him when he found out Brent had slept with her, knowing that Jordan's tough exterior hid a gentle soul, a soul that found purpose in devoting herself to running the free clinic in the rough part of town.

Since that night back in September when she threw him out of her life, Brent had been functioning on autopilot. He dialed her number from memory, frowning when he got her voice mail. "Dammit, Jojo. Jax is going out of his mind with worry. Call him, or I'm showing up at your door. You call me, and I'll turn around and head home."

He ended the call, pulled back out onto the highway, now fully awake from the fear and resulting adrenaline, and switched to the southbound highway at the next interchange. He had to get to the south side of Indianapolis to find out why she wasn't answering her phone. He shoved the worry away and concentrated on the drive.

His eyes burned from lack of sleep as the sun dropped below the horizon when he exited the interstate and slowed to make the turn onto the county road. He was always surprised how dark it was out away from the city. The stars twinkled as he drove down the deserted road, the barren fields on either side the only witnesses to his journey. He slowed for the turn into the driveway by habit. The three months he spent living there with Jordan were the best of his life; then she threw him out.

The house was dark, but her car was parked in front of the garage. *It's only seven thirty in the evening. She should still be up. Why are all the lights out?* His "cop sense" told him something wasn't right. His stomach cramped with worry.

After shutting the car door softly, he stopped and listened trying to pinpoint what was bothering him. No barking. Where was Sadie? He knew she would normally be barking like crazy at the sound of a car in the drive. The crunch of snow beneath his cowboy boots echoed in his ears as he crept closer to the front porch. He pulled out his cell phone and dialed 911 when he saw the front door swinging in the breeze. After identifying himself and explaining the situation, the dispatcher told him to hang back and wait for backup to arrive.

He crept up the porch steps and into the house with his gun in one hand and his flashlight in the other; following orders had never been high on his list of priorities. Methodically making his way through the house, he cleared each room on the first floor before heading up the stairs and doing the same with the guest bedrooms and bath.

Silently slipping through the door of the master bedroom, he stopped at the sight of a small pool of blood at the foot of the bed. It shone black as ink in the beam of his flashlight as his heart thumped faster and his stomach rolled. A trail of blood drops led him to the walk-in closet where he found the desk chair shoved under the doorknob locking it from the outside.

After carefully moving the chair, he opened the door and swept the flashlight beam through the closet, stopping at the sight of Jordan standing in the back corner with a baseball bat in her hands covered in blood.

"Jordan? It's me, Brent."

Her eyes looked through him, wide open and terrified. He stepped back as she swung the bat, stumbling forward and landing on her knees with a sob. "Stay back, please," she said, her voice cracking.

"Jojo, it's me, Brent. Is that your blood, baby? You can put down the bat. I won't hurt you."

She blinked as if waking from a deep sleep. "Brent? Thank God it's you!" She stood using the bat to pull herself upright. Stepping toward Brent, she stumbled, and he caught her in his arms.

He could feel her trembling as she wrapped her arms around him. "Where are you hurt?" he asked as he pulled out his cell phone to call 911 again and request an ambulance.

"It's Sadie's blood. We have to get her to the vet." She pulled herself out of Brent's arms and knelt in front of the puppy. "He stabbed her in the side of her neck. I got the bleeding under control, but I don't know how bad it is…" A hitch in her voice cut off the rest of the sentence. "I didn't have my bag, so I couldn't do much."

Brent dropped to one knee and reached out to pet Sadie. "Hey, girl. We're going to get you fixed up soon."

Sadie's tail beat a staccato rhythm against the floor as she licked his hand.

Brent pulled a blanket off a shelf in the closet and wrapped Sadie up before carefully picking her up to head downstairs. The golden-haired cocker spaniel snuggled into him, her tongue swiping his cheek.

"Police. Don't move!"

Chapter Two

THE CLICK of the handcuffs startled Jordan out of her mental fog. "What are you doing? I keep telling you that Brent didn't do anything." After trying to convince Jax over the phone she was fine, she was in no mood for any problems.

"Don't worry, Jordan. They're just doing their job. Now, use my cell and call the vet. I've got you parked in, so take my car and get Sadie the attention she needs. When you get back, I'll have this all sorted out."

Jordan felt like her whole world was coming apart at the seams. Sadie needed the vet, Lainie was in the hospital, Jax was freaking out, and Brent was being treated like a criminal for helping her.

Why doesn't anyone understand?

She called Sadie's vet and explained the situation, planning to meet the vet at his office. She ended the call and set Brent's phone on the kitchen table in front of him. "Maybe if I explain to them again…"

"No. Go get Sadie to the vet. I'll be fine. They're just being cautious. I'll have it handled by the time you get back."

Jordan kissed his cheek and whispered, "We'll talk later."

6

One of the officers picked up Sadie and carried her out the door behind Jordan.

Brent slumped in the chair, finally letting the picture of Jordan covered in blood fill his mind. "Shit. I'll never get that out of my head," he whispered to himself.

His mind flashed to the other horrid image he wished he could extricate from his memory: the vision of her shaking, terrified, huddling in the bathtub after she had been targeted by a killer searching for Jax's wife. She had suffered a PTSD-like episode brought on by her fear. Comforting her had turned into an intense kiss, eventually landing them in bed together. Somehow, after more than a year, he had talked her into giving their relationship a chance. For three months, they were happy living together in her house outside of Indianapolis until she became moody and withdrawn, hiding phone calls and texts, making him wonder if she was seeing someone else. When he confronted her about it, she threw him out.

Enraged at his inability to get through to her, he left and moved far enough away that she wasn't a constant distraction. Being the heir to the Halston fortune, he had plenty of money to live wherever he wanted. He found Fairfield Corners, a small town about two hours north of Indianapolis, where he could be Brent and not Marshall Halston or Mitchell Brent Halston, majority stockholder of the Halston Group. It was a quiet town, and it was only twenty minutes from Fort Wayne where Jax and Lainie had relocated.

"Mr. Halston, I'm sorry we had to handcuff you, but you know it's procedure. I just got off the phone with your former supervisor, and you've been cleared." The officer unlocked the cuffs and set them on the table. "We have your cell number if we have any follow-up questions."

Brent rubbed his wrists. "Okay. I will be taking Ms.

McKenna up to Fort Wayne to be with her brother and sister-in-law. We can be back here in about two hours if needed."

After the officers and crime scene investigators left, he stepped over to the front window and looked out over the driveway, frowning at the yellow crime scene tape. "Damn right we're going to talk when you get back, Jojo. Living without you isn't working for me anymore, so you're just going to have to get used to me in your life again."

He verified that the front door was locked up tight before heading for the stairs. Jordan would want to be headed to Fort Wayne as soon as she returned from the vet, so Brent packed her suitcase with everything she would need for an extended stay. No way was he letting her come back here alone.

Jordan pulled into the driveway, relieved to see the police cars were gone. "Looks like your daddy was right, Sadie. I hope he got everything straightened out okay." Sadie whined when she picked her up. "Let's go see your daddy, baby girl. I'm sure he's worried about you."

Setting Sadie down in the grass, Jordan fumbled with Brent's key ring, smiling when she saw he still had the key to her house. After carrying Sadie in the house, she set her next to her food dishes. "Are you thirsty, Sadie? I'll get you some fresh water."

Jordan busied herself filling the water dish, wondering if Brent was upstairs. Lost in thought, she didn't notice Brent walk into the room fresh from a shower. She turned with the water dish in her hand to set it in front of Sadie when she noticed him out of the corner of her eye. Startled at his sudden appearance, she dropped the dish and let out a scream.

"Jesus, Brent. Make some noise next time, will you?" She

frowned at him leaning against the counter as if he belonged there. He was wearing an old pair of Jax's sweats and the T-shirt she had kept when she threw him out. The shirt hugged him like a second skin, reminding her how he kept himself in shape. *He would still belong here if you weren't such a scaredy-cat. Leaving wasn't his idea.* His brown hair was slicked back, but she knew it would soon become unruly as it dried.

"Sorry, Jojo. I thought you heard me. So, how's Sadie? What did the vet say?"

"She'll be okay. Luckily, it wasn't too deep. He stitched her up and gave me some pain meds and antibiotics."

"Oh, thank God." His arms went around her, holding her close with his nose in her hair. "Go take a shower, and then we can get out of here. Your bag is already packed except for your bathroom stuff."

Jordan opened her mouth to make a snide comment about him taking over her life and decided against it. He knew she would want to get to Fort Wayne as soon as possible, so he packed for her. No big deal. "Thanks, Brent. Give me about fifteen minutes, and I'll be ready to go."

"No problem, Jojo," he said to her back as she walked out of the room.

She walked into the master bath and found the towel he had used hanging neatly on the rod, and his clothes were in a bag on the counter. He was neat, almost to a fault. Her friends complained about how their husbands or boyfriends couldn't manage to get their dirty clothes off the floor and into the hamper or that they constantly left the seat up. That had never been one of their problems.

As the hot water beat on the back of her neck, she let herself remember the good times, pushing away her anxiety and dread. They would have plenty of time to talk about why she threw him out. Hopefully, he would be able to forgive her for her stupidity.

Knowing he had a two-hour drive ahead of him, Brent popped a pod in the coffee maker and started it brewing. When his cup finished, he poured it into a to-go mug and started another, not that they would need the caffeine once they started talking.

Sadie whimpered and licked his toes, reminding him that he needed to get his bag from his car and change clothes. Finding his T-shirt in Jojo's drawer had put a smile on his face. He knew she still cared. It had been at the top of the stack of T-shirts; she obviously had worn it recently.

The rumble of the shower stopped, bringing his attention back to Sadie. "Come on, girl. You can do your thing while I get my bag from the car." After slipping on his boots, he picked her up, carried her outside, and set her in the grass, praising her when she relieved herself.

Grabbing his bag from his car, he brought Sadie back into the kitchen and set her on the blanket in the corner that was her bed. He knelt and nuzzled her face. "I'm glad you're okay, girl." A single tear ran down his cheek and into her short, golden fur at the thought that he almost lost both of them that day. *If I had remembered to charge my phone, maybe I could have prevented the whole incident.* "I'm sorry I wasn't here to stop him."

Jordan stopped at the bottom of the stairs when she saw Brent kneeling in front of Sadie. Her heart twisted when she saw him wipe a tear from his face. It always startled her when he showed emotion. In public, he was stoic, never showing his emotions as he went about his job and daily life. But behind closed doors, he showed her a side of himself that he kept hidden from everyone else, for some reason wanting the world to think he was a womanizing loner.

She cleared her throat and walked into the kitchen, wanting to give him a chance to pull himself together.

"You ready to go? I already made coffee. All I have to do is put your bag and my dirty clothes in the car. Sadie's things are already loaded." He picked up the stack of clothes he had brought in from the car. "Just give me five minutes to change."

"Brent, I…" She took a deep breath and finished her thought. "Thanks for coming to our rescue. And for driving us to Fort Wayne. You could have left and let me drive myself, so thanks."

Jordan looked at the floor when Brent brushed his fingers over her lips. "You don't realize what I feel for you, Jojo. I would never expect you to make this drive by yourself when you've had such a traumatic day."

He picked his keys up from the table and jingled them in his hand. She knew that was sometimes the only way he would show he wasn't as calm and cool as the façade he showed the world.

After changing in the guest bath, he stowed the rest of the bags in the trunk. He leaned against the car and waited as she locked the door, watching as she walked toward him, his eyes half-closed against the glare of the porch light.

She hoped he couldn't see the fear she felt.

Chapter Three

BRENT GLANCED at Jordan as she sipped her coffee, wondering what she was hiding. He was sure she had lied to the police when giving her statement. "You going to tell me what really happened, Jojo?"

"What do you mean?"

"I know you didn't tell Officer Melton the truth about what happened. What did you hold back?"

"Nothing. Just drop it, Brent."

"Dammit. How do you expect the police to catch the perp if you don't tell them the truth? What are you scared of?"

"Nothing."

He looked over and caught her trying to stifle a sob. Whipping the wheel to the right, he pulled off the road. As soon as he parked, he pulled her to him, wrapping his arms around her as she sobbed. The scenarios running through his mind made him grind his teeth as he waited for her to pull herself together. *What if he touched her?* Pushing that thought out of his mind, he wiped the tears off her face and looked into her eyes. "Did he touch you? Is that what you held back?"

"God, no. I wouldn't lie about that."

Relief flooded through him. He could see in her eyes that she was telling the truth. "Then what? What didn't you tell the police?"

He watched as she took a couple of breaths before answering.

"I lied when I said I didn't know who it was or what they wanted."

"What? Why would you lie about that?" He wanted to grab her and shake some sense into her. "Was it one of your patients? Dammit, Jojo. I told you it was too dangerous for you to work at that clinic."

"No, it wasn't a patient." She covered her face with her hands. "It was Chad."

"What the hell? Why wouldn't you tell the cops it was that asshole? Oh wait, don't tell me. He didn't mean to do it. Just like he didn't mean to hit you all those years you were married?"

He shoved his door open and stood, his anger making him want to punch something. Striding down the berm, he remembered Jax's complaints about Jordan's douche canoe of a husband. If only they'd known about the abuse at that time, maybe they would have been able to do something about it.

He stared down the road at the horizon, rubbing his neck to relieve the tense muscles as he willed himself to calm down. Reminding himself this was his opportunity to reestablish his relationship with her, he shoved his anger away.

His temper back under control, he returned to the car. "Sorry." He ran his hands through his hair. "No, I'm not sorry. You know how I feel about that asshat. I'm sure you think you had good reason to lie, and I hope you'll tell me." He started the car and pulled out onto the highway.

"You must be exhausted. We've got another hour to go, so why don't you try to sleep."

Jordan stared out the windshield. "Thanks for not prying. I guess I owe you for that, too." She looked into the back seat to check on Sadie and then closed her eyes.

Chapter Four

BRENT PULLED into the driveway and rolled to a stop. He watched Jordan sit up and rub the sleep from her eyes.

"Are we at the hospital already? Feels like I just fell asleep."

"No. I needed to make a stop first. I didn't want to leave Sadie in the car by herself, so I made a slight detour to a friend's. Don't worry. They'll take good care of her."

"I want to meet them."

"No problem." He opened the door to the back seat and picked up Sadie. "Come on, Sadie girl. Time to make friends. You'll love the kids."

The door opened before he stepped onto the porch. Adam Bricklin stood in the doorway and chuckled at the look on Jordan's face when she recognized him. "So, you obviously didn't tell her about your famous neighbor."

As they trooped through the door, Jordan unsuccessfully kept the look of shock off her face. She smacked Brent on the arm. "Why didn't you tell me you knew Adam Bricklin?"

Adam's wife, Ragan, walked into the room, a fussy AJ in her arms. "Brent, what brings you here so late? And who's this cutie?" She held the back of her hand out for Sadie to sniff before scratching the dog's ears.

"I need a favor. This is Jordan and Sadie. Jordan is Jax McKenna's sister."

"Good to meet you, Jordan. Jax was a big help to us a while back."

"We ran into a bit of trouble this evening, and I need somewhere to leave Sadie where I know she'll be safe and comfortable for a couple of hours. I hate to impose, but you were the first ones I thought of."

Ragan handed the cranky baby to Adam, who immediately quieted in his father's arms. "I wish I knew how you did that," she muttered under her breath as she held her hands out for Sadie. "Oh, you're hurt."

"She's okay. She's been to the vet and has been stitched up. We need to get to the hospital in Fort Wayne to see Jax's wife; they had a scare with her pregnancy today, and Jax needs his sister."

"Of course," Ragan replied. "You don't even have to ask."

After giving Ragan the pain meds and the vet's instructions, they left to go to Fort Wayne.

Once they were back on the road, Jordan looked at Brent in wonder. "How did you meet Adam Bricklin? I loved his last album."

"They're my neighbors. I own the house to the north of theirs."

"That huge two-story with the pole barn out back? Where did you get the money for that?"

"You're not the only one with secrets. I'll tell you the whole story tomorrow. Right now, we're almost at the hospital."

After parking the car, they strolled into the lobby, Jordan pulling at his hand as if that would make him walk faster.

"Relax. Everything's fine. Jax would have called if anything changed."

"I know. I'm just anxious to see for myself."

After a short ride in the elevator to the third floor, they walked down the hall toward Lainie's room. The door opened, and Jax walked out, closing it quietly behind him.

"Jackson," she cried, and she ran up to hug him.

"Hey, little sis. About time you got here."

"Has there been any change? I want to talk to her doctor. Where's her chart?"

"Relax. They have Lainie's blood pressure under control. They ran some tests, and hopefully we'll know what happened in a couple of hours." He hugged her, looking over at Brent with a nod. "Now, what is going on with you? Do the police have an ID on the guy who broke into your house? And how's Sadie?"

"Sadie is fine."

Before she could make up a lie about what happened, Brent interjected. "It was her asshat ex."

"What?" Jax roared, earning him a glare from a nurse. "I thought you had a restraining order."

"You know those generally aren't worth the paper they're printed on. She hasn't told me the whole story yet—but don't worry, she will. That asshat is going to jail for a long time for this."

Jordan put her hand on Brent's arm. "I'm going to check on Lainie. Why don't you get us some coffee."

As soon as the door to the hospital room clicked shut, Brent started pacing the hall. "Has she said anything to you about Chad? I don't think this was an isolated incident. Whatever's going on? I'm fairly certain it's the reason she threw me out." He rubbed his eyes; the adrenaline from finding her in the closet covered in blood had long since dissipated, leaving him exhausted. "Let's get that coffee. My ass is dragging."

Paper coffee cups in hand, they found an empty waiting room. Gulping his drink, Brent thought about how to explain how he found Jordan without Jax freaking out.

"Tell me everything. I knew she was lying about something when I talked to her on the phone, but I thought there was more damage to the house or something, not that it was Chad."

"Jojo's fine. You saw that for yourself, and Sadie just needed some stitches. As soon as I got out of the car at the house, I just knew something was wrong. I called it in, but I couldn't wait for backup. I cleared each room, and when I got to the master bedroom, I had that burst of adrenaline you get when you know it's close, whatever it is. I thought the blood pool at the end of the bed was bad, but opening the closet door to find her wild-eyed and covered in Sadie's blood, I don't think I'll ever get that picture out of my head."

"Fucking hell." Jax paced the length of the room and back. "I knew I should have taken care of him when I found out he was hitting her, but I let her talk me out of it." He rubbed his hands over his face. "I'm glad it was you who found her."

"The worst part of all of this is I think he's been harassing her for a while. Why else would she start hiding phone calls and texts and then kick me out with no explanation?"

"I think you're right. Can you convince her to make another statement and tell the whole truth?"

"Yeah, I'll get her to do it if I have to drag her there kicking and screaming; which, knowing her, is a distinct possibility."

Finally convinced that Lainie's blood pressure was under control and the baby was in no immediate danger, Jordan agreed to go back to Fairfield Corners with Brent.

Standing behind him at the front door as he unlocked it, she looked around marveling at the size of the house and the yard.

"Wow, it's even bigger than it looked from next door. Can you afford this?"

"Don't worry about it. I've got it covered. How about a quick tour before we get some sleep?"

He showed her the kitchen and family room, walking past the rest of the rooms which sat empty.

"Why don't you have any furniture in the other rooms?"

"With this last case being in Louisiana, I haven't had time. The furniture here is what I put in storage when I moved into your place. Don't worry. I'll sleep downstairs on the sofa. It's comfortable."

She was glad to be following him up the stairs so he didn't see her cheeks turn pink at the thought of sleeping in his bed. Missing him had become a dull ache, always there waiting to expand whenever something reminded her of him.

Chapter Five

THE GURGLE of the coffee maker pulled him from sleep, and the scent of the fresh brew encouraged him to open his eyes. He looked around and wondered why he was sleeping on the sofa instead of upstairs in his bed until Sadie's cold nose touched his arm reminding him of the events of the previous evening. "Morning, Sadie girl. Where did you come from?"

Yawning, he stretched and shuffled toward the kitchen and its promise of fresh coffee. Jordan stood at the stove, putting bacon in a skillet to cook.

"Morning, Jojo. How did Sadie get here?"

"I hope you don't mind. Adam called, and I answered your phone. Since I was up, he brought Sadie over about thirty minutes ago."

"Of course, I don't mind. I've missed having her wake me up with her cold nose." He ruffled the fur around Sadie's ears. "Did you sleep well?"

"Surprisingly, yes. Your bed is incredible. What kind of mattress is it? I need to get one for my bed."

He poured a mug of coffee, sipping the dark brew as he sat on one of the stools at the breakfast bar. Watching her make breakfast had been the best part of his morning when they were together. "Has Sadie been out?"

"Yes, and I've already changed her dressing this morning. The stitches look good. No sign of infection."

"Good. Now, we need to talk about what happened yesterday."

The spatula slipped out of her hand and clattered on the floor. "Let's have breakfast first," she said as she picked it up and placed it in the sink.

"Okay, but then you're going to tell me what's going on. I know it's more than just what happened yesterday."

"What about you? Are you going to tell me how you can afford this house?" She flipped the eggs onto two plates and turned off the burner. "And why did you buy such a big house?"

They ate in silence, Jordan pushing her food around on her plate.

"Are you going to eat that or play with it?" he asked with a frown. "It looks like you haven't eaten a full meal in a while."

"Why do you make me losing weight sound like a bad thing?"

"Because I still care about you. Did you think throwing me out was going to change that?"

She scraped the remains of her breakfast in the trash can. "Finish your breakfast. I'm going to take a shower."

Before he could comment, she was halfway up the stairs.

He dried the frying pan and hung it on the pot rack. Needing a shower himself, he went upstairs. He couldn't help but notice she had left the door to the master bath cracked, and he could see her partially dressed in her jeans and a bra, drying her long, dark hair into its customary waves. Her back was splotched with bruises, all where they would not show when she was fully clothed. Unable to contain the rage they invoked, he stormed to the door and yanked it fully open.

"Brent? What are you doing?"

"What the fuck, Jojo? How long has he been hitting you?" He noticed how some were fresh and others looked weeks old. His hand traced one of the newer bruises, his fingers barely touching her skin.

"Don't touch me," she implored him as she turned to face him, trying to cover her exposed skin with her hands and arms as her cheeks blazed with embarrassment. She grabbed the shirt she had slept in and pulled it on.

"How long has this been going on? This is why you threw me out, isn't it?" He ran his hands through his hair, trying to calm their shaking. The sorrow in her eyes squeezed his heart making it hard for him to breathe. Pulling open a dresser drawer, he grabbed a pair of sweats and pulled them on before grabbing a T-shirt and socks, his face hard as granite as he imagined choking the life out of her ex.

"Brent? What are you doing?" Her sorrow had turned to fear. "Where are you going?"

"How long have you been sleeping with him?"

All the color drained from her face, and she looked as if she might be sick. "You think I let him do this?"

"Well, didn't you? Isn't that what all the lying and phone calls and texts were about? You were letting him touch you while we were still together?"

He was sitting on the bed tying the laces on his running shoes when she whispered, "How can you think I would let him do this. He blackmailed me."

His breakfast threated to come back up as his stomach churned. "Jojo, baby, this was more than blackmail. He raped you." The thought of her ex's hands on her, hitting her hard enough to create those bruises, circled in his mind, blotting out everything else. "Why didn't you tell me?"

She turned her back to him and rubbed her hands up and down her arms. "He threated to have my license pulled if I didn't cooperate. He took pictures while we were married without my knowledge. In one of the pictures, it looked as if I enjoyed his sick sex games rather than disgusted by everything he made me do. He told me the girl he'd brought in was underage and that I could be arrested as an accomplice. When that didn't work, he threatened to go to the board and have the funding for the clinic pulled. I couldn't take the chance he would actually do that, so I started to meet him at the motel down by the highway."

He came up behind her, pulling her back to his chest, hugging her to him. "You don't have to worry. He will never touch you again." Kissing the top of her head, he whispered in her ear, "I love you, Jojo."

When he let her go, she turned to look at him. "Where are you going?"

"We need to call Officer Melton. They need to put out an APB on Chad."

"Won't they need a signed statement or something?"

"Yes, and we need to document your bruises. Let me take some pictures with my phone, and we can go into town and have the sheriff take your statement."

The fear in her eyes made him want to skip the formalities and go find Chad and beat him until his face wasn't recognizable as human. "Don't worry. I'll be with you every step of the way. Sheriff Marsten and Deputy Miller will take it slowly."

"Are you sure?"

"I'm sure. Now, lift your shirt up in the back so I can photograph your bruises."

When they parked in front of the sheriff's office in Fairfield Corners, Jordan started to tremble.

"Hey, it's okay. Nothing to be afraid of here. You know that."

"What if they don't believe me?"

"Why wouldn't they believe you? Because you're a woman? No worries, Jojo. James and Logan will believe you."

She dabbed at her eyes with a tissue and made sure her lipstick was still perfect before she flipped the mirrored visor up. "Okay, let's get this over with."

They walked up to the reception desk, and Maureen exclaimed, "Marshall Halston, you must be the reason James and Logan are jumpy this morning. You've got the same look on your face. You can go on into the conference room, and I'll let them know you're here."

He squeezed Jordan's hand when she started to pull away. "Don't worry. Everything is fine. Try to relax."

"Yeah, right."

He watched her face as Sheriff Marsten and Deputy Miller walked in and closed the door behind them.

"Has anyone ever told you that you look like Adam Bricklin?"

The guys all chuckled, and Logan winked at her. "He's my cousin."

Brent watched as Logan's southern drawl worked its magic on Jordan, putting her at ease as he explained the process.

James pulled Brent aside while Jordan was occupied with Logan. "I took a look at the photos you sent. We'll do whatever we can to help."

"Thanks."

Their attention returned to Logan and Jordan, and they started the process of taking her formal statement.

Jordan fiddled with her watchband as they started the recorder.

"First, tell us in your own words what happened yesterday."

"Well, uh…"

James pulled his chair closer and put his hand over hers. "It's okay. We aren't going to judge you."

"I'm sorry. I'm just so nervous. I've never really talked to anyone about this. I feel so ashamed I never stood up to him."

"Would it be easier if Logan and I left? You can give your statement to Brent."

"God, no." Her cheeks bloomed red. "I…"

"Would you be more comfortable without Brent in the room?"

She picked at her thumbnail. "Yes," she said softly.

Brent stood and tried to smile before kissing the top of her head. "I'll be right outside if you need me, Jojo."

When the door closed behind him, he resisted the urge to turn on the intercom so he could listen in as she gave her statement. It would be hard enough for him to read her statement, but to hear her recount what happened, he didn't think he would be able to hear her talking about it without punching something.

After pouring a cup of coffee from the pot, he found a chair facing away from the interrogation room and slumped into it, his mind a jumble of thoughts. He rubbed his eyes and tried to clear his mind of the memory of her covered in Sadie's blood. He leaned back in the chair and closed his eyes. The first time they met was burned into his memory.

He had convinced his partner and fellow US Marshall, Jackson "Jax" McKenna, to go out on the town to celebrate the big bust they had made that day. Their hard work had paid off with ten suspected drug dealers charged and in jail. Riding high on the adrenaline of the bust, he ordered shots of tequila and coerced Jax into downing a couple. Mellow from the buzz of the alcohol, he didn't mind the beauties snuggled up to him. He loved women but would never let himself love one woman. He was content with being a bachelor. And then she walked in the door—a dark-haired beauty with soulful eyes and a body that fueled all his fantasies.

He stared as she walked toward them, his eyes riveted on her face. His blood pumped faster as she walked closer. When she tapped Jax on the shoulder and stepped into his arms, he almost punched his friend.

Jax took her hand and pulled her toward the table. "What are you doing here, Jordan?"

Jordan? This is his sister?

God, he was doomed.

She looked at Brent and smiled. "Chad is out of town, so I decided to come out for a drink."

"What do you want to drink? It's on me."

"Margarita on the rocks with salt."

Jax turned toward the bar and then turned back. "Jordan, this is my partner, Brent Halston. Brent, this is my sister, Jordan." He punctuated his introduction with a pointed look at Brent.

Brent stared back at his partner. He didn't know why Jax was giving him that look. He had already warned him away from his sister. "Hey, Jordan, nice to finally meet you." When her hand touched his, he had to remind himself to breathe.

"Oh, so you're the famous Brent I keep hearing about. You can put your tongue back in your mouth, lover boy. Jax has told me all about you and the revolving door on your bedroom."

"Jax exaggerates."

"Tell that to the two ladies hanging on you right now."

"We were just celebrating a big bust."

"A big bust? Whose? The blonde's or the redhead's?"

"Ha ha ha. Funny."

He gulped his beer, trying to quell the fire racing in his blood. She was the most beautiful woman he'd ever seen, and she affected him like no other. The two girls hanging on him, and they were girls compared to the woman standing in front of him, faded into the background. His focus had settled on Jax's sister, and he couldn't tear his gaze away from her. Lips begging to be kissed and chocolate brown eyes that snapped with attitude, why did he think he needed the badge bunnies who had latched onto him as soon as he walked into the bar?

"Just wanted to get that out of the way. I'm married, and I don't need to be fending off advances from you."

"Do I detect a note of jealously in that statement?"

"Never."

Two long years later, Jax had called him out of the blue, asking him to check on his sister.

Lost in his memories, he jumped when he felt Jordan's hand on his arm.

"Brent? You okay?"

"Yeah. Just resting my eyes. You ready to go?" The urge to hit something came back when he saw the tears in her eyes.

She dug around in her purse and pulled out a tissue. After wiping her eyes, she balled up the tissue in her fist. "I wish he would just leave me alone."

Chapter Six

JORDAN'S STOMACH rumbled loudly as they walked out of the sheriff's office. "How about some lunch before we go to Fort Wayne? Sadie is at Adam and Ragan's, and I'm sure the kids are spoiling her, so we don't have to rush back home."

"Sounds good."

He pulled into the drive-in and parked. "I recommend the burgers, and you have to get the onion rings. They are worth the drive."

"Okay. And a chocolate shake."

"Good choice." He drummed his fingers on the steering wheel as he waited for the carhop.

"So, when are you going to tell me your big secret? What don't I know about you, Brent Halston?"

"Later. I promise I'll tell you when we get home tonight."

She let the matter drop, but he could tell she wasn't happy about it. Staring out the window, she didn't say a word to him until they arrived at the hospital and found Jax getting Lainie ready to go home.

Jordan rushed over to Lainie. "How are you feeling?"

Brent pulled Jax out into the hall. "Is everything okay with the baby?"

"Yes. Thank God. Now, what's going on with Jordan? Did she give an amended statement?"

"Yes." He reached into his inside jacket pocket and pulled out the copy of her statement James had made for him. "I haven't been able to make myself read it yet."

"You still love her, don't you?"

Brent looked down at his shoes and rubbed the back of his neck. "Yeah."

Jax scanned the paper, the worry lines on his forehead getting deeper the farther he read down the page. "He better not show himself to me. I can't guarantee I won't kill him for this."

Brent took the papers back and shoved them into his pocket. "I'll read it later."

The door opened, and Jordan maneuvered Lainie's wheel-chair out into the hall. "Let's get going. I want Lainie home and in her own bed resting for the next couple of days."

"Yes, Mother," Jax replied sarcastically. "That's exactly what Lainie's obstetrician advised. You know I'll do my best to keep her calm. I don't want to make another trip to the emergency room."

Jordan hugged her brother. "I know you will. I'm just so relieved this was a false alarm." She pushed the wheelchair toward the elevator. "Come on, guys. Let's get a move on."

After getting Lainie settled in and comfortable, Brent took Jordan back to his house in Fairfield Corners. He scooped coffee into the coffee maker, hoping the brew would help him get through what he wanted, no needed, to tell Jordan. Knowing he had been lying to her about something so major had been eating at him, but the time had never been right to discuss it. Once they both had full coffee mugs and the sugar and creamer was within reach, he dove in and started talking.

"Well, to start, my full name is Mitchell Brent Halston, and I lied when I told you I wasn't related to *those* Halstons. When my father died, I became the majority stockholder in The Halston Group."

Jordan stared at him, her hands around her mug. "I don't understand. Why would you lie about who you are? Did you think I would treat you differently if I knew you came from money?"

"Actually? Yes."

She folded her arms across her chest, and her chin lifted. "Well, I guess now I know how you really feel about me. I'll pack, and you can take me to the nearest motel." She stomped up the stairs and slammed the door. *The nerve of that man, playing me for a fool. He probably thought it was fun to go slumming with the altruistic doctor. Screw him!*

The door flew open and bounced off the wall leaving a divot in the drywall from the doorknob. "As usual, your first reaction is to run away before you even know the whole story. If I didn't love you so damn much..." His voice trailed off, and then his hands were on her arms and his lips were on hers, hungry and searching.

She tried to push away from him but he was stronger. "How dare you! Get your damn rich lips off of me." Unable to move away, she kept her head back trying to keep her lips as far away from his as possible. "Let me go. I won't be anyone's plaything."

His hands let go of her arms. "Is that what you got out of what I just told you? Sometimes I wonder what goes on in that brain of yours, Jojo. How did you come to the conclusion I was only playing house with you?"

"Well, weren't you? Why else would you be with

someone like me?" She returned to the bed, folding clothes and placing them in her suitcase.

"Jojo, look at me." When she turned to look at him, the tears shimmering in her eyes ripped his heart out of his chest and threw it across the room. "God, baby, don't cry. I can handle your temper and your sass, but your tears, they rip me apart." He sat on the bed and rubbed his hands through his hair, making it stand up in spikes. "I knew I was going to screw this up. Will you please sit down and hear me out? I'll take you to the bed and breakfast in town afterwards if you still want to leave."

Silently, she sat on the bed as far away from him as she could get without falling to the floor. "Okay. Talk." She looked down at her hands, avoiding his gaze.

With a finger under her chin, he brought her gaze up to his face. "Hey, I would never do anything to hurt you. Please believe that."

"Why should I believe you? You've been lying to me since the beginning." Her temper flared. "Does Jax know?"

"Yeah, he knows."

"Dammit! You even had my brother lying for you. You're no better than Chad."

"Now, you wait just a damn minute. If you let me explain…"

Her gaze sliced through him sharp as a knife. "No. Take me to the B&B. Now." She threw the rest of her clothes into the suitcase and closed it. "Do you know if pets are welcome? If not, Sadie can stay here with you."

"I'm sure she will be able to stay with you. I know the owner, and she's an animal lover."

They sat in silence as he navigated the small-town streets. She held onto Sadie, her hands feeling the warmth of the puppy's body as she stared out the window. *How could he lie to me? How do I always end up in this situation?*

As soon as he parked next to the restored Victorian house, she bolted out of the car, leaving him to bring in her suitcase. She stopped just inside the door, her eyes wide in wonder. The house had been decorated for the upcoming Christmas holiday. White lights were entwined with greenery swags and draped around the windows, doors, and the large fireplace. The faint strains of Jingle Bells added to the festive atmosphere.

Brent followed her into the house, her suitcase in his hand. "Jordan, will you please listen to me?"

Straightening her back, she turned to face him when the proprietress hurried into the room.

"I'm so sorry I wasn't here to welcome you." Glenda DeHaven moved to the registration desk, her eyes focusing on Sadie. "Oh, she's beautiful. What's her name?"

Relaxing at the older woman's inquiry, she put her purse on the counter and set the pup on the floor. "This is Sadie. She's had an exciting couple of days. I hope having her with me is not a problem."

Glenda crouched to give Sadie a chance to sniff her hand before ruffling her ears. "Oh, Sadie is not a problem at all. Hello, Mr. Halston. Will that be one room or two?"

"Just one," Jordan replied. "He's not staying." With a wave of her hand, she dismissed him. "You can go now." She turned away and busied herself with the checking-in process. She didn't see how his shoulders slumped at her abrupt statement.

Brent paced the porch, too keyed up to get behind the wheel. He watched through the window as Jordan followed Mrs. DeHaven up the stairs. He stared out at the snow-covered lawn for some time. When he shivered from the cold, he paced the length of the porch and back. "What the hell do I do now?"

"You're going to wear a path in the floorboards if you keep pacing like that."

He turned to find Glenda standing in the doorway. "Sorry. I'm just... Oh, hell, I don't know what."

"Come in out of the cold and have some tea. You can tell me why your lady friend was glaring at you as if she wished she could strangle you."

He followed her into the house through the lobby to the kitchen. "I screwed up. I thought I was protecting her, but it backfired."

She bustled around the kitchen, putting on the kettle and gathering the makings for tea and transferring cookies from the cookie jar on the counter to a plate. "Is she the one you told me about? The doctor?"

"Yes. I found out why she threw me out, and I can deal with that. The problem is I lied to her about who I am. She puts on a brave face, but I know how vulnerable she really is. I let her believe I was just a cop, the same as her brother, and now she thinks I did it to take advantage of her."

She busied herself with the teapot, setting it on the table to steep. "So, basically, you backed yourself into a corner and you don't know how to fix it." Turning back to the cupboard, she picked up a couple of plates.

"You could say that. I knew she would be upset when she finally found out I have money, but I never expected her to think I was using her."

"There's more to it than just that, isn't there? Didn't you tell me her ex-husband comes from money?"

He crumbled a cookie onto his plate. "Yes," he growled. Just thinking about what his Jojo had gone through made him want to lash out at the world. "She was still married to that sorry excuse of a man when I first met her. From the way she and her brother were talking, I had a feeling there was some emotional abuse going on in the relationship. The day I found out it was physical…" Just saying it out loud made him want to vomit. How could someone treat his precious Jojo like that? Another cookie was reduced to crumbs in his fist. "I know I can't fix what he did to her, but I don't know how to get her to see me and realize I'm not like him. She needs to understand that having money does not make someone abusive."

Glenda took his hand and brushed the crumbs onto his plate. "Give her some time. She's feeling vulnerable and betrayed. I'm sure she'll come to see you're nothing like the man she married, that the only similarity is the money." She checked the teapot. "Here, have some tea," she said as she poured some into his cup. "Let that warm you up a bit."

He wrapped his fingers around the cup, surprised at how delicate the cup looked in his hands. In a way, it reminded him of Jojo; it looked delicate, but it was strong just like she was. He took another cookie and actually ate that one, enjoying the chocolate melting on his tongue. Now that he was warm, his outlook on his relationship with Jordan looked just a bit brighter. He would convince her somehow that they belonged together.

Chapter Seven

IT HAD BEEN three days and numerous text messages, but there had been no word from Jordan. How was he supposed to convince her of his sincerity if she wouldn't talk to him? The burn of the scotch temporarily took his mind off the sad state of his love life as he watched the party. He had planned to skip the holiday event at his neighbor's until Jax informed him Jordan would be there. When he walked in, she ignored his presence, her gaze sweeping over him as if he weren't there. Draining his glass, he set it on the bar and picked up the bottle.

"Brent, glad you could make it," Adam said with a grin. "When are you going to go over there and talk to her?"

"Not any time soon. Believe me, she hasn't had time to get over being mad."

He laid his hand on Brent's shoulder. "Don't wait too long. The longer it goes, the harder it is to get back to a good place, especially when there are secrets involved. Believe *me*, I know that from experience."

"You and Ragan? But you two are so happy now."

"Remind me to tell you the story sometime, but not now. This is a party. Try to enjoy yourself."

Brent picked up his drink and sipped, his mind turning over Adam's words as he stared across the room at Jordan. He gripped the glass tighter as he watched her laugh with Fletch Carmichael. The hand gripping his heart squeezed tighter when she brushed the hair off his forehead, her eyes soft.

He closed his eyes and inhaled slowly, trying to calm his racing thoughts. No way would she move on that quickly, not with the threat of her ex-husband hanging over her head. Watching the singer flirt with Jordan pissed him off; she shouldn't be fawning over someone else while he watched. Gulping the rest of his drink, he slammed it down and grabbed the bottle, intending to refill the glass. He watched as Jordan laughed at something Fletch said, her hand on his arm.

The bottle in his hand, he strode toward the back door and the patio, which he hoped was deserted. White twinkle lights were draped on every available surface, giving the night a fairy-tale quality. His thoughts immediately went to how much his Jojo would love the solitude and the lights. Normally, she wouldn't feel comfortable at a party, but obviously Fletch was the cure for that.

Taking a swig of the alcohol, he wondered how he ended up chugging scotch out on Adam's deck all alone in the freezing cold with a holiday party going strong on the other side of the French doors. Tomorrow was Christmas Eve and he was alone—again. Cursing his last name and the money and position that came with it, he sat on the retaining wall and stared out across the yard at his house. The light and warmth from the party inside highlighted the difference between this house and his. He had bought his house for Jordan, not that she had noticed in the short time she had stayed there. One night and he had managed to piss her off even more than usual just by telling her the truth. No lights or Christmas decorations in sight, his house looked as empty as his heart felt.

Lost in his thoughts of Jordan, he hadn't heard the door open or Ragan's footsteps on the frozen flagstone patio. "Brent? What are you doing out here by yourself?"

His brain fuzzy from the alcohol, he blurted out, "I couldn't stand to see her flirting with another guy. Feels like she dug my heart out with an ice cream scoop and threw it on the ground and stomped on it." After another pull on the bottle, he continued. "I want her to be happy but I'm not ready to watch her happy with someone else."

She pulled the almost empty bottle out of his hand when he raised it to take another drink. "So, your solution is to sit out here alone and get drunk and slowly freeze to death? Sounds like a great plan to me." She raised the bottle to her lips and drained it. "And just so you know, she's doing a great job pretending to be happy. Just so you know, Fletch is a flirt but he's in a relationship with a friend of mine. If I had any doubts about his feelings for Nikki, I would be in there putting a stop to it."

"You just had a baby. You're not supposed to be drinking." His hazel eyes turned hard. "I thought you were different." He turned away from her and stared out across the yard.

"What? What do you mean?"

"I knew a good time was more important to my mother than I was, but I thought you were different. I was actually jealous of Adam having you in his life, but now I see the truth."

She reached up and grabbed his earlobe and twisted.

"Ow! What the hell?"

"Since you're obviously drunk, I'll let that comment

slide. Not that it's any of your business, but that is the first drink I've had since I found out I was pregnant."

He slumped over, his head in his hands. "God, how did my life get to be such a mess? I thought I was protecting her by lying, but all I did was drive her further away."

Ragan sat next to him and put her hand on his arm, remembering a night at the pub when she had consoled him when he drank too much and told her the whole story. "She's still mad about the money, isn't she? It's only been a few days. You need to give her some time to realize you are not her ex."

"I don't know if that will ever happen. I knew my money was going to be an issue. That's why I didn't tell her. Now she's got it in her head that I thought I was slumming the whole time we were together." He rubbed his hands up and down his face. "Why can't she see how much I love her?" he mumbled as he stared at his feet.

"She's blinded by her anger. You just need to wait it out. She'll eventually see how you feel about her." Standing, she brushed at the back of her skirt. "You need something to take your mind off your problems. What are you planning to do now that you're no longer a US Marshall?"

"I don't know. Maybe I'll figure out something that will get rid of this damn money. It's nothing but a giant pain in the ass."

"The money isn't the real problem here; Jordan's inability to see the truth is." Noticing his drooping eyelids, she continued. "Why don't you go home and sleep it off. Things will look better in the morning when you're not staring at the world through a haze of alcohol." Pulling at his hand, she steadied him when he stood and swayed.

"Thanks for keeping me from turning into a drunken hermit, Ragan. I hope Adam realizes just how special you are." Pulling her into a hug, he prayed that someday he would be able to make Jordan see the truth about his feelings for her.

"Go home and sleep it off. Call me when you get to the house or else I'll send out a search party to find your drunk ass."

Jordan stared unseeing at the Christmas tree, the image of Brent with his arms around Ragan permanently burned into her brain. She had convinced herself to give him a chance to explain, but the sight of him in Ragan's arms crushed her heart. "I knew it," she whispered as she blinked rapidly to keep the tears at bay. "Asshole."

She turned and hurried toward the front door, her coat and purse forgotten as all she wanted to do was go back to the B&B where she could sob in private. Her eyes on her feet, she didn't notice Fletch in her path, a frown on his face. "Hey, beautiful. What's wrong?"

The concern in his eyes blew away her last shred of control. A hand at her mouth to hold in the sob that wanted to escape, she ran around him toward the door. Wrenching it open, she didn't feel the cold air hit her, her only thought to get away from the happiness and the people. Realizing she didn't have her keys, she resigned herself to going back in, at least long enough to grab her purse.

Fletch stood in the doorway, his arms crossed on his chest. "What's wrong?"

"My life is such a mess. I need to get out of here. Do you have your keys?"

"What about your coat? Don't you want to say goodbye to Adam and Ragan?"

"No," she sneered. "I don't ever want to see her again. Never mind. I'll walk back to town."

Putting his hand on her arm, he frowned when she flinched. "Who hurt you?" he growled. "Was it someone at the party? Tell me who, and I'll take care of them."

"Oh God, no. It wasn't someone here. It was a long time ago." She didn't want to admit she had been fooled by Brent once again.

Visibly relieved, he pulled his keys out of his pocket. "Let me take you home. You're staying at the B&B, right?"

"You don't have to do that. I'm much calmer now. I'm sure I'm okay to drive." She turned to make her way back into the house, her progress halted by a pissed off Fletch.

"No. I said I will take you home, and I will. Besides, I'm staying there, too." With his hand at her back, he steered her back into the house.

While she dug through the pile of coats on the bed, Fletch sent a text to Adam telling him he was taking Jordan back to town and he would talk to him in the morning.

In the light of the room, he noticed the purple shadows beneath her eyes.

Something was definitely wrong, and he wanted to fix it. His inability to help as he watched his mother's spiral into mental illness drove his need to fix everything.

Chapter Eight

JORDAN WOKE to a world that was too bright. Her eyes felt hot and swollen and as if they were full of sand. Rolling over to get away from the sun shining in through the open curtains, she discovered a warm body next to her in the bed. Still half asleep, she wondered when Brent got there and curled up next to him.

An hour later, she surfaced from sleep once again. Blinking to bring the world into focus, she found a bearded face, not the clean-shaven face of Brent she expected.

"Morning, beautiful."

"Oh, shit." She scrambled across the bed, falling to the floor when she scooted off the side of the mattress.

"Hey, you okay, Jordan?" Fletch asked as he stretched.

"Oh my God. I'm no better than he thought. You have to leave. Now."

He stared at her and laughed.

"This isn't funny! No wonder he was hugging Ragan. I'm a slut. Jumping into bed with a guy I just met."

"And don't forget the fact that I have a girlfriend," Fletch said with a chuckle.

She sat on the floor and put her head in her hands. "He was right to go slumming with me. I'm not worthy of a guy like him."

"Hey, that's enough of that kind of talk. I'm sorry. I let my mouth run off before my brain kicked in. God, I'm worthless before my coffee." He picked her up and sat her on the bed. "Look at me, Jordan. Nothing happened. You cried yourself to sleep and I was too tired to get up and go to my own room."

She stared out the window, not hearing him. "I don't deserve him. He was right. I don't deserve a decent guy."

"Jordan! Look at me." He sat next to her on the bed. "I don't ever want to hear you say you don't deserve a decent guy. Was it that Brent guy who put that idea in your head? He should be shot." He picked up his jeans, grinning at the sight of her in his T-shirt. The hem hung halfway to her knees.

"God, no. Brent's a good guy."

"Then why aren't you with him?"

"He comes from old money, the kind that normal people like us will never see. Lunching and committees and fundraising aren't for me."

"You're judging him based on the fact one of his ancestors made a lot of money? That's a pretty narrow view and you're probably way off base."

"I don't think so. He's better off without me." She looked down and blushed when she realized she was wearing his T-shirt. "I'll just go change so you can have your shirt back."

"Keep it as a souvenir. Someday, you'll look back on this and laugh. Or you can sell it on eBay for a bunch of money."

"Oh, I would never do that." She stood and then reached down to pick up her dress. When she felt the sting of his palm on her butt, she dropped to her knees and covered her head with her arms, hoping he wouldn't hit her where it would show. "No! Please don't hit me!" she cried.

Sadie whined in her crate, scratching at the door to get out.

With a crash, the door to the room swung open with such force it bounced back toward the hulking figure in the doorway. Brent's hands were curled into fists, his eyes focused on Fletch. "Get away from her, you asshole!"

Stunned, Fletch stood there, not understanding what was happening. When Brent's fist connected with his face, he stepped back and put up his hands. "What the hell, dude?"

Brent grabbed Fletch by the throat, his rage blocking out everything but the memory of her cries.

"You never lay your hands on a woman. There is nothing she could do that would deserve that."

Jordan's sobs penetrated the rage, pulling his attention away from Fletch. A bright red handprint showed on Fletch's neck, testimony to the grip Brent had had on him.

Brent dropped to his knees in front of Jordan, and he reached out to brush the hair off her forehead. "Jojo, look at me, baby. Did he hurt you?"

Her eyes cut right through him; she was still reliving the past.

"I swear, all I did was playfully swat her on the ass and she freaked out." Fletch stepped back when Brent stood.

Pulling the blanket off the bed, Brent wrapped it around her. He picked her up off the floor and sat on the bed with her in his lap. His heartbeat started to return to normal when she looked up and threw her arms around him, burrowing her face in his neck.

"What the hell was that all about?" Fletch asked, his voice raspy.

"I think she has PTSD. Her ex-husband is an abusive

asshole who thought beating on his wife was totally accept-able." He kissed the top of Jordan's head, afraid to let her go.

She sat up and wiped at her cheeks. "What happened?" When she spied the handprint on Fletch's throat, she gasped and then looked up at Brent. "Did you do that?"

"I heard you cry out and all I could think about was getting to you. It's all kind of a blur. What the hell is he doing in your room, anyway?"

"You have no right to ask me that. We are not together." She jumped off the bed to dig through the clothes in her suit-case, grabbing a sweater and jeans. "I want you gone by the time I get out of the shower." She knew Brent would think she had slept with Fletch but she didn't care. She just needed him to leave. The bathroom door slammed, making him jump.

Shoulders slumped, Brent stared at the closed bathroom door.

Sadie howled as if she sensed his distress.

"Aw, Sadie girl, it's okay." He reached down and unlatched the door to her crate. "Do you need to go out?"

He followed Fletch out the door, Sadie pulling on the leash.

The memory of her cries tore at his heart as he watched Sadie run around the back yard. Sadie did her business and looked up at Brent expectantly.

"I know. You're ready for your breakfast. Let's get you back upstairs before your mom gets out of the shower." He picked her up and held her closely. "I hope I can convince her to give us another chance," he said to Sadie, leaning his head against hers.

After filling Sadie's bowl with food, he returned the leash to the top of the dresser and left the room, closing the door softly behind him.

Each step he took down the hallway and away from his Jojo felt like walking through wet cement. How was he supposed to get her to change her mind when she wouldn't even talk to him?

"You're lucky I don't go back on tour until the middle of January. Damn. You have a hell of a right hook."

He looked up to find Fletch standing in the doorway to his room, his hands in his pockets.

"Is Jordan okay?"

"Yeah. She's back to being mad at me again."

"Why don't you come in and tell me why she's so pissed at you. I just put the coffee on."

With a nod, Brent followed him into the room.

Fletch picked up a mug and poured coffee into it from a carafe. "You want a cup?" At his nod, he poured another mug and handed it to Brent.

"I want to apologize for what happened." He grimaced at the red mark in the shape of his hand on Fletch's throat. "And especially for that. But I still want to know what you were doing in her bed." He realized he had curled his free hand into a fist just thinking about another guy being in bed with Jordan.

Fletch took a seat on the couch in the sitting area, looking right at home despite the Victorian-era furniture. He motioned for Brent to sit and sipped his coffee before he started. "Something upset her at the party last night. I caught her as she was ready to walk back to town without her coat or purse. I couldn't let her leave alone in that condition. Do you have any idea what happened?"

"No. I spent most of the party out on the patio getting drunk. If I'd stayed to watch her flirt with you, I don't know what would have happened. Probably similar to what happened this morning." He looked down into his mug as he remembered what it felt like to watch his Jojo flirt with someone else. "Despite my former occupation, I'm not a violent guy; but something about her brings out the caveman in me."

Fletch pulled out his phone and scrolled through the photo gallery until he found a picture of Nikki. "I get that. If anyone hurt my Nikki, real or imagined, I don't know if I'd react any differently." Turning the phone so Brent could see the picture, he continued. "I met her while I was here at Thanksgiving; she's all I think about."

"If this Nikki is so important to you, why were you flirting with Jordan?"

"Nikki had to stay in California and work, and the rest of the band scattered for the holiday, so I flew out here to sign some paperwork with Adam." He sipped his coffee before continuing. "I noticed a beautiful woman who looked like her whole world had collapsed. I was just trying to get her to smile and laugh. I figured a little flirting would do the trick, and it did."

Brent poured himself some more of the dark brew. "I hate seeing her so sad. If I could get her to sit down and listen to me, I'm sure I could get her to understand why I lied about my family's money."

Fletch looked up with interest. "Your family has money? That explains some of what she said this morning before you burst in. She was mumbling something about not being good enough for a guy like you."

Brent got up and paced. He needed an outlet for the anger that was building. "Her ex comes from old money. His family wishes they were worth as much as I am. Damn. I knew I should have killed him when I had the chance."

"So, just how much are you worth?"

"Somewhere in the billions. I don't even care how much."

"You're right up there with that Halston guy who inherited all that money a couple of years ago."

"You could say that since I am that Halston guy."

Fletch grinned. "Small world. My grandfather, Gabriel Mason, is on the board of directors of the Halston Group."

"Shit. You probably know her ex, Chadwick Washington. God, even his name is pompous."

Fletch scowled. "I've met that conceited asshole. That he is abusive does not surprise me. Please tell me she took him to the cleaners."

"No. She got nothing other than her car. You have to understand Jordan; she didn't want to relive what he did to her, but now it looks like she's not going to have a choice. I just recently found out he's been blackmailing her for months, and he's the reason she threw me out of her life three months ago."

Fletch walked over to the window and stared out across the snow-covered yard. "I knew I didn't like that asshole. Please tell me she's going to press charges this time."

"There is a warrant out for his arrest, but he was tipped off that the cops were coming for him. He's been off the radar since last Sunday; if Jordan knew, she would be petrified." He rinsed out his mug and set it on the counter. "I need to get her somewhere out in public so I can talk to her. She won't want to make a scene."

"I can help with that. I'll get her to take me to lunch at Adam's pub to apologize for what happened this morning. I'll leave the table to take a phone call or something, and you can sit down and talk it out with her."

"It's worth a shot."

Chapter Nine

THE NEXT DAY, Brent watched the pub floor from his vantage point in Adam's office. Possible scenarios ran through his mind as he jingled the keys in his pocket. This had to work.

Even knowing Fletch brought Jordan to the pub, seeing her laugh at something Fletch said twisted his guts until it felt as if he couldn't breathe. If they hadn't planned this little misdirection, he would be fuming at her smile for someone else. Letting them get comfortable, he waited until they had ordered before calling Fletch's phone.

With a wink, Fletch answered his phone and apologized to Jordan as he stood to leave the table.

Jordan's attention was on the waitress serving their drinks when Brent slipped into the chair across the table from her. "Hi, Jojo."

"What the hell do you want?" she whispered. "I told you we were done."

"No, we're not done until you listen to me. I've let you get away with being mad about what you imagine I did to you for too long."

She gulped her wine, setting the empty glass on the table with a thump. "What do you mean by that?"

"It means you are going to sit here and listen, really listen to what I'm saying."

"No. I don't think so." She stood, her chair screeching across the floor. "I don't want to listen to anything you have to say." She looked at him wide-eyed when he stood and grabbed her arm. Even with the anger she could see in his eyes, his grip was firm but not hurtful. "Let go of me. You're causing a scene."

"You don't want a scene? Fine." He strode across the floor, pulling her behind him. Fletch met them at the door with her coat and purse.

"Fletch, don't let him do this, please." Her eyes widened when he shook his head. "You two planned this. Ganging up on a helpless female. You should be ashamed."

At Fletch's laugh, she grabbed her coat and pushed her arms into the sleeves. "Well, let's get this over with so I can get back to the B&B."

Fifteen minutes after he shoved her in his car, she stomped up the front steps and waited for him to unlock the door. His hand at her back, they entered the silent house.

She was surprised when he led her to the family room. What had previously been a big, empty space was now filled with comfy looking furniture and a huge flat-screen television. There was even a Christmas tree with a wrapped gift under it, and plush stockings hung on the mantle.

"You've been busy. It looks nice."

"I'm glad you approve. Now, sit." He tossed their coats on the chair and led her to the couch. Frowning at her attempt to scoot as far away from him on the sofa as possible, he looked at her and sighed when she checked the time on her phone.

He grabbed the offending device out of her hand, set it to silent, and put it on the end table. "Now that there are no distractions, you are going to listen."

"I don't know why you think a conversation is going to fix what you did. Why don't you just take me back?"

"No!" he roared. "Dammit," he mumbled as he paced the length of the room and back. "What do you see when you look at me? Now that you know who I am, you look at me differently. You want to know the reason I lied to you? That's why. I'd been half in love with you for two years before we got together, but I knew if I told you about the money, you would refuse me on principle."

He sat and rubbed his hands over his face. "I... Shit. I didn't want to lie to you, but after what that asshat put you through, I knew it skewed your thinking about people coming from old money." Running his hands through his hair, he continued. "I know I didn't show it at first, but that first time I met you, I knew you were different. My reputation was another hurdle. Convincing you I was sincere and not just looking for an easy score terrified me."

She snorted. "You? The legendary Brent Halston terrified? Yeah, right. Why would you be terrified of me?" The window reflected her face back at her. "I thought we were past the lies when you moved in, but we weren't. And that was a big one."

"I grew up with a mother who let the money take over her life. She turned to alcohol when she couldn't deal with the hangers-on and the social station required of a Halston. When my dad died, she gave in to the booze and used it as a shield. I was ten when I realized the alcohol had taken over. She would routinely leave me alone in the house for days at a time. At least Maria was there; the cook was a better mother than she was." He sat on the couch and hung his head. "I guess what I'm trying to say is that I don't know what a loving relationship looks like. I love you, Jojo, but I don't know what to do about it. I feel like this is our last chance to work things out."

She snuck a peek at him, frowning at the exhaustion she could see in his eyes. "I want to forgive you, but I don't know if I can."

"When you threw me out, I drove around the state looking for somewhere that felt comfortable. As I drove past this house, I knew this was it—the house that we were meant to share. I bought it for you. That's why there was no furniture. I was waiting for you to come back to me so we could buy everything together. When you found out the truth and wouldn't talk to me, I bought some furniture and even set up a Christmas tree."

Standing behind her, he wrapped her in his arms as she continued to stare out at the snow-laden landscape of his back yard. "Can you at least think about forgiving me? I don't want to live without you anymore." He kissed the side of her face and backed away. "I'll take you back to the B&B and let you have some time to think. Just let me get your gift." He picked up the wrapped box and handed it to her. "Even then, I wouldn't give up. Every piece of furniture was picked with you in mind."

Shrugging into her coat, she turned and caught him watching her, a wistful look on his face she'd never seen before. Images of her ex and his abuse fought with the memories she had of the short time Brent had lived with her. Her temples throbbed with a headache brought on by the stress of the last few days. She would think about what he had revealed to her today after a nap and some aspirin to deal with the pain.

The silence in the car was deafening as they both thought

about their conversation. Lost in memories, she didn't notice the car coming at them.

"Hold on, Jojo! This idiot's going to hit us!"

Brent swerved, and the other car hit the driver's side door, pushing them off the road into the ditch. The car slid down, landing in the bottom of the ditch with a thud, bouncing on the shocks.

The ticking of the engine as it cooled was the only sound as she opened her eyes. Mentally taking stock, she wiggled fingers and toes, relieved she didn't seem to have received any serious injuries. A groan from Brent reminded her she wasn't alone in the car. She fumbled with the seatbelt, cursing until the buckle finally parted and she could turn and check on him.

"Brent? Can you hear me? Don't move until I check for injuries." The cold air blew across her face from the shattered window bringing the sound of a car door.

Brent's eyes focused on her. "You okay, Jojo? Are you hurt?"

The pain in his gaze worried her. "I'm fine. Just a little banged up. Nothing a hot shower and some pain reliever won't fix. What about you? Where does it hurt?"

"I'm fine. But be careful. I don't think that was an accident."

The crunch of boots on the snow took her attention from Brent to the man leisurely walking toward the car, his hands in his pockets. The way he walked looked familiar, but dusk was settling in bringing the darkness, and she couldn't get a good look. She couldn't worry about that now. She needed to make sure Brent was okay.

"Quit lying, and tell me where it hurts, tough guy." She tried to act like nothing was wrong, but the pallor of his skin worried her.

"It's my leg, and it's stuck. I can't move it."

"Let me see if I can get your door open. Maybe then I can see how bad it is." She climbed out of the car and looked up into the face of Chad. "What do you want? Was it you that hit us?"

He grabbed her arm and dragged her around to the driver's side of the car where she could see Brent struggling to free himself. "Of course, I did. You keep forgetting you belong to me."

"I don't 'belong' to anyone, especially not you!" she yelled as she pulled out of his grip.

He stumbled forward and winced at the sudden movement. Glaring at her, he smiled.

She put herself in between him and the car, trying to shield Brent.

"You have belonged to me since the day you said 'I do'. When will you get that through your stupid brain? You can't hide from me. I'll always find you." The hand that had been in his pocket now held a gun and it was aimed at Brent. "As soon as I take care of your boyfriend, I'll have to remind you again what happens when you disobey me."

She cowered against the car, the memories of past beatings running through her mind.

"You're stronger than that, Jojo," Brent whispered. "Don't let him win."

She straightened, squaring her shoulders and stared back at Chad. "No more. You can't do this to me anymore. I'm putting a stop to it right now. I'm strong, and I'm smart. I don't need you to tell me how to act or how to live. I won't do it anymore."

His eyes turned hard. "You really forgotten what happens when you defy me? Stabbing your mutt wasn't convincing enough? I guess I'll have to kill your boyfriend to make you realize I'm serious." He raised the gun and glared down the barrel at her.

She looked him in the eye and prepared herself to protect Brent. She couldn't let anyone else get hurt because she chose to marry the wrong guy. "You'll have to go through me. My mistake is not going to hurt anyone else." She could hear Brent struggling to extricate himself from the car behind her.

"Dammit, Jojo!" he yelled. "Get away from him." After a couple of deep breaths to tamp down the pain, he yelled again. "You hurt her and I'll hunt you down." He pushed the car door open, freeing his foot from the mangled metal.

"Brent, I've got this. Chad can't control me anymore." She turned to her ex, her face showing her determination to protect the man she loved.

"You pull that trigger, you're a dead man. Place the gun on the ground and kick it over to me."

She looked past Chad and saw Deputy Logan Miller standing behind him, gun drawn and face stoic. As her ex obeyed the officer's command, she turned back to Brent, shocked to discover him standing next to the car, his face ashen. "Brent, sit down before you fall down. What the hell did you think you were going to do? No way was I going to let him shoot you."

He swayed drunkenly, mumbling something she couldn't hear. More police cars pulled up, and she heard the wail of an ambulance siren. He resisted when she took his arm and tried to lower him to the ground, putting his foot down. "Fuck. That hurts." He groaned as his knees buckled, and he dropped to the ground.

"What is it with you and Jax thinking you're invincible?" she grumbled as she assessed his ankle, knowing it was broken before she even touched it. "This is broken. Standing on it might have made it worse." She blinked back tears as she realized what she had done: she had stood up to Chad.

Brent pulled her into an embrace. "Don't ever scare me like that again. When I saw him point the gun at you and I couldn't help, I thought I was going to lose you again." He buried his face in her hair, taking the time to get his emotions under control.

"No way was I going to let him shoot you. Protecting you became more important than anything he could do to me. I finally understood what my heart has been trying to tell me." She brushed his hair off his forehead and kissed him. "I love you, Mitchell Brent Halston."

He shifted and let out another curse word when it jostled his ankle. Hating to see him in pain, she let her medical training take over. "I need to immobilize your ankle, and it's probably going to hurt," she said in her doctor voice as the EMTs rushed over to them. "I need a splint for this ankle."

The emergency room was organized chaos. The snowfall had caused a multitude of small traffic accidents. Jordan sat in the waiting room outside the imaging department. She pulled her coat closed and shivered, the events of the day finally catching up with her. She had finally stood up to her ex and had saved the love of her life in the process. She was reliving every mean comment she had made to Brent over the last week, even practically throwing her gift back in his face as she walked out to the car at his home.

"Why do I deserve such commitment?" she mumbled to herself as she wondered if the gift was still in the car or if it was lying on the side of the road at the site of the accident.

"Jordan? You okay?"

She looked up to find her brother standing in front of her. Jumping up, she hugged him, burying her face in his chest.

"Why did you let me be such a bitch to him? He almost died because I couldn't see what was right in front of my face. All I could focus on was what Chad did to me." She sniffled and tried to keep the tears in her eyes from falling.

"Hey, he's fine thanks to you. I'm so proud of you for standing up to Chad." He hugged her closely. "And I'm relieved that you will finally have him out of your life for good." He pulled some tissues out of his pocket. "Here, dry your tears and tell me why you're crying. It's over. Everyone is safe and Chad is in custody."

"I've been such a bitch to him, and he still loves me. Who does that?"

"You better be talking about Brent," he said with a smile.

"Of course, I am. God, who else would it be?" She looked up and saw his grin. "You're an ass."

"Anything to make you smile, little sis." He brushed her hair out of her face. "He really loves you, you know."

"I finally see that. I can finally see past the money." She blew her nose and wiped her eyes. "Oh shit. The present. I need to get back out there and find it. I hope it didn't get ruined in the accident." She stood and zipped up her coat. "Can you give me a ride?"

"No."

"What do you mean, no?"

"There's no need for you to go back out there." He pulled the small, wrapped box out of his pocket. "Brent made me promise to find it and make sure you got it. Go ahead. Open it."

"No. I want to open it with him here."

"He told me to make sure you opened it now and not to wait. Don't make me break a promise."

She picked at the tape, not wanting to rip the paper. "I

know. I know," she said when she saw the look of impatience on his face. "I've almost got it." She peeled the paper away from the box carefully, something in her wanting to keep it as a memento. She gasped when she saw the necklace nestled in the box. The pendant was one-half of a heart enhanced with diamonds. "Why half of a heart?"

Jax pulled an envelope out of his pocket. "This will explain. I'm supposed to let you read this in private. I'll go check on the status of Brent's x-rays while you read it." He stepped over to the desk to talk to the clerk on duty.

Her hands shook as she turned the envelope over and saw her name scrawled on the front in Brent's handwriting. Tears threatened again as she opened the envelope and pulled out a folded piece of paper. Unfolding the paper, she began to read.

My dearest Jojo,

If you're reading this, it means I was successful in finally getting you to forgive me for being an ass. That first day we met and you ignored my advances, I fell hard. I didn't know it then, but it became clear later. No other woman compares to you. No one. Moving in with you was the happiest day of my life. I had no idea what I had done to deserve the love of a woman like you. Even after you threw me out, I still loved you.

No matter what happens in this life, I will always love you.

This necklace is a physical reminder that you hold half of my heart in your hands, FOREVER.

. . .

Always, my love,

Brent

PS... If you're ready to take a chance on us, look in the box under the necklace.

She gently pulled the necklace out of the box, cursing at the tiny clasp as she struggled to get it hooked behind her neck. Ignoring the impulse to check how it looked, her attention went back to the box. Of course, she was ready to take a chance on them now that she was out from under Chad's control. She frowned at the thought of her ex, disgusted with herself that it took so long for her to stand up to him.

Her hand trembled as she pulled at the cardboard that held the chain, revealing the real treasure: another note, this one small enough to fit in the bottom of the box.

Jordan McKenna, will you marry me?

Taped to the note was a diamond solitaire ring.

The squeak of a soft sole against the tile floor distracted her from the box in her hand. Tears wet her cheeks as she looked up to find Brent sitting in front of her in a wheelchair, his eyes filled with pain and hope.

"Well?" he asked. "Is it going to be me and you against the world, Jojo?"

She nodded her acceptance, the lump in her throat not allowing her to vocalize her feelings.

Jax plucked the box out of her hand and handed it to Brent before he pulled his phone out of his pocket. He snapped pictures as Brent slid the ring on her finger.

She leaned into Brent and kissed him, whispering "I love you" against his lips. When she straightened up and looked into his eyes, she could see the pain buried under the happiness, and her medical training took over. "Let's get you back to the ER and get this ankle taken care of."

Chapter Ten

ONE WEEK LATER...

New Year's Eve arrived faster than Jordan had hoped, but somehow everything was in place for the wedding later that night at the B&B. She was fuming at her groom-to-be. He was being stubborn about being in a wheelchair during the ceremony. The surgery on his ankle had been a success, but he wasn't supposed to put any weight on it for another two weeks. With a call to the surgeon, they had come to a compromise: he could stand but only if he used crutches, and would go back to the wheelchair as soon as the ceremony was over. They weren't even married yet, and already she wanted to strangle him for being stubborn.

Still decorated for Christmas, the Victorian mansion would be perfect for their small wedding. Jax and Lainie would be standing up with them, and only a few people had been invited: Adam and Ragan Bricklin, Fletch Carmichael was bringing Nikki Romero, and Sadie, of course. Their reception would be a dinner in the private dining room at the B&B, catered by Glenda DeHaven.

The last week had been filled with shopping for a dress and keeping Brent off his feet. She had to admit, the Halston name got things done. She had found the perfect dress online at a boutique in New York City but didn't want to buy it without trying it on. Brent had arranged the Halston jet to fly her to New York and back the same day. The vintage Grecian style dress swept the floor. With its long sleeves and a touch of lace, it nipped in at her waist and accentuated her in all the right places—it was perfect. She had kept her room at the B&B to use for planning the wedding. Being onsite made it easier.

Keeping Brent off his feet wasn't as easy. She wished the doctor hadn't given him crutches. He was constantly going up and down the stairs, unable to relax and let his body heal. She had threatened to tie him to the recliner to get him to stay in one place for more than ten minutes at a time. That had lasted for a couple of hours before he was up and out the door.

Jax had shown up earlier, offering to keep Brent occupied while Lainie helped with her dress and handle the final details. Now that everything was in place, she had a few minutes to relax before she had to start getting ready. Lainie was sitting in the chair next to the fireplace with her feet up, her hands resting on her belly.

"Do you want kids, Jordan?"

"Yeah, I guess I do. I prayed every night I was with Chad that I wouldn't get pregnant, but now that I'm marrying Brent, I hope we can start a family right away. Any particular reason you're asking?"

"Just something Jax said the other day. He told me he caught Brent staring at me. He almost went ballistic until he realized he wasn't looking at me like he wanted to kiss me or anything; it was like he was staring at me in wonder. He got the strangest look on his face when I placed his hand on my belly and he felt the baby kick."

Jordan frowned at the door when they heard a knock. Tightening the belt of her robe, she turned to open the door. "Yes?"

The tall, thin, young man looked at her hair and grimaced. "I'm Michael. Mr. Halston flew me in to do your hair and makeup. May we come in?"

"Oh, I don't need any help. I was just going to do my hair as I normally would. And I don't wear much makeup."

Michael forced his way into the room, followed by a woman loaded down with bags. "Oh, my dear, you don't need to worry about a thing. Michael will get you all dolled up and looking beautiful in no time."

"What do you mean you'll make me beautiful? Brent loves me just the way I am. He's not expecting some pampered princess."

"Don't worry. You will still look like you, only more polished. You have fabulous cheekbones. Now, let me see your dress. I hope to God it's not some horrendous fru-fru creation with tons of lace. That wouldn't do for you at all. You need something classic."

Lainie unzipped the garment bag and brought out Jordan's dress for his inspection. "I think you'll be pleasantly surprised, Michael."

Jordan looked at her in surprise. "You know him? Is he always this pushy?"

"Yes, and yes. Brent had me video chat with Michael to be sure he was the right one to do your hair and makeup. He doesn't think you need improving. He just wanted you to feel pampered today."

She looked from Michael to Lainie. "Well then, I guess we better get started."

Another knock at the door had her muttering under her breath. "What now? At this rate, I'll never be ready."

Michael's assistant opened the door for Glenda to walk in with a bottle of champagne. "Jordan, I figured you could use a little refreshment before the ceremony. I'll get this open and poured. I've also got a bottle of sparking grape juice for the mother-to-be. Don't want to leave anyone out."

Jordan looked around and wondered what had happened to her plan to relax before she prepared herself to get married. Michael took her hand and pulled her to a chair and motioned for her to sit.

"Now, I don't want anything too outlandish."

"Have no fear, my dear. You are in good hands." He began wetting her hair with a spray bottle.

She jumped when she heard the snick of scissors. "Hey, what are you doing?"

"Don't worry. I'm not cutting off much. Just putting in some layers and trimming the ends. When was the last time you had your hair trimmed?"

"I've had a busy couple of months. It wasn't high on my list of priorities."

"You're going to love it. Trust me. Lainie, tell her it's going to be fine."

Lainie giggled. "You don't know who he is, do you? Michael is one of the most sought-after hairstylists in Los Angeles. It can take months to get an appointment with him. Relax and enjoy it."

"Okay, well in that case, make me beautiful." She gulped the champagne in her glass.

Two hours later, she had been plucked, powdered, and coiffed.

"Can I look yet?" she asked grumpily. "It's almost time, and I haven't even had a look yet."

Michael pinned the wreath of flowers into her hair and declared he was done. He motioned for his assistant to place the full-length mirror in front of Jordan.

"Close your eyes, and no peeking."

"Oh, all right. I've gone along with you this far."

Once the mirror was in place, he helped her to stand. "Okay, open your eyes and gaze upon the wonder that is a beautiful bride."

She was almost afraid to look…almost. She gasped. "Oh my." Her hair was swept up in the back showing off the curve of her neck. A few tendrils were artfully arranged to highlight her face. She looked like herself, only prettier. "How did you…? Oh, never mind. I'd never be able to duplicate it anyway."

Turning to Michael, she hugged him. "Thank you. I feel like a princess."

"You're welcome. Now, I want you to promise you'll find someone good to keep your hair trimmed. If I hear you've let it get out of control again…"

"Oh, don't worry. I'll keep up with it. Promise."

The alarm on her phone chimed signaling it was time for her to take her place at the top of the staircase.

"Oh, that's my cue," Lainie stated as she picked up the smaller bouquet of flowers. "Let's get you married. The sooner we get this done, the sooner you can get Brent off that ankle."

"That's true. Let's do this."

With a quick hug, Lainie stepped out onto the landing at the top of the staircase. Jordan waited for the music to change to signal it was her turn to float down the stairs.

Brent shifted the crutches under his arms, trying to find

where they were the most comfortable. Maybe the wheelchair wasn't such a bad idea after all. He watched as Lainie slowly walked down the stairs, her pregnancy evident. *Soon*, he thought as his stomach twisted in knots. What if she changed her mind? They'd overcome so much to get to this point that he didn't know if he'd survive another rejection from her. Contemplating what he would do if she had backed out, he looked up when the music changed.

He swallowed, willing the contents of his stomach to stay where they were. He'd never been this nervous, not even in the middle of a gunfight with a gang of drug smugglers. A foot clad in a white pump stepped down onto the staircase, and he thought he would pass out from a lack of oxygen. He looked at Jax when he felt his hand on his shoulder.

"Breathe, dumbass. Don't need you falling on your face."

With a whoosh, his lungs remembered what they were supposed to do. He looked up again and almost dropped one of the crutches to Jax's delight. Unable to look away from the vision of his Jojo in a white, floor-length dress, he waved his hand at his friend to quiet his snickers. *God, what did I do to deserve this woman?*

The ceremony passed in a blur. He couldn't take his eyes off his bride. He thought he responded at the proper places, but he wasn't sure until he heard the judge say, "You may now kiss the bride."

She leaned into him. The world dropped away when she put her lips against his and kissed him. When he shifted to get a better angle, she whispered against his lips, "Don't you dare put any weight on that foot."

He smiled. "There's the Jojo I love. Sassy as ever." He gazed into her eyes, thanking God for whatever he'd done to deserve to have her in his life.

Gratefully, he sat down when he felt the wheelchair touch

the back of his legs. He hadn't realized how draining it would be to stand and keep his weight all on one foot. Pulling on her arm, he sat his bride on his lap and wheeled them toward the dining room amid the laughter of his friends.

"See, I've got it figured out already. Kiss her senseless and then move her where I want her to be. No problem."

"We'll see about that, Mr. Halston. That could work both ways."

He grinned as she bent and kissed him again. "Thanks for taking one last chance on me," she said when she came up for air.

"Always."

Also by L.A. Remenicky

https://www.lavishpublishing.com/authors/l-a-remenicky/

Saving Cassie (Fairfield Corners Book 1) - Everyone has secrets. Sometimes secrets can get you killed. After ten years in the big city, Cassie Holt is moving back to her hometown to take over the bookstore left to her by her beloved Gram, vowing to live her life alone. To her best friend, Sheriff James Marsten, Cassie seems to be the same girl that left Fairfield Corners to go to college but Cassie has secrets and one of those secrets could get her killed. When one of her secrets becomes a threat to her life, James turns to his new deputy to help him keep Cassie safe. Deputy Logan Miller has been burned by love and is not looking to get involved with anyone anytime soon. When he is thrown into close quarters with Cassie, the sparks begin to fly and he begins to see through the walls Cassie has built around her heart. As the threat gets closer, can Logan protect Cassie and protect his heart? (Mature Adult, 18+)

Ragan's Song (Fairfield Corners Book 2) - It only took one look into his eyes for Ragan to know she was in trouble. Adam Bricklin has heard the melody in his head for years, the melody that told him if a decision was right or wrong. When he met Ragan Newlin, the song told him she was the one. Devastated when circumstances tore them apart, it has taken three years for him to finally move past the heartbreak. With a new girlfriend, a new album in the works, and his daughter doing well in school, things are looking bright; until the day Ragan returned to Fairfield Corners bearing secrets that could change their lives forever. (Mature, 18+)

Loving Jessie's Girl - Fiercely independent, Rina Abbot hid her true situation from everyone, including her best friend, Jessie. Out of money and unable to care for her rescue dogs she had no choice but to accept the help of the handsome stranger with a familiar face. Afraid to trust him, she tried to ignore the feelings he stirred within her as they searched for his missing brother...

Preacher's Redemption - With the past and the present on a collision course can their love survive?

2nd Chance Valentine - A chance encounter in a bar with the one who got away had Cam Beckett dreaming of his own happily ever after. But, only if he could convince Kara to forget their disastrous first date and give him a second chance.

My Grumpy Valentine - Ashley Sweet was living her dream— baking cupcakes and making plans to expand her bakery—until Thorton Hodges walked in with an offer she could, and did, refuse.

Hawk's Last First Kiss - Would Sadie be Hawk's last first kiss?

Christmas Grump - Stuck together in her tiny house, would the Grump ruin her holiday mood?

Quin to the Rescue - Rescuing her cat from a tree was only the beginning.

A Whisper Through Time - Will Jaya choose love or peace?

Heart of a Tin Man - Can the heart-hardened Tin Man save Dorrie and her little dog too?

About the Author

Romance author, dialysis warrior, furkid mom, and Best Fiends addict. Lover of coffee, 80's music, and all things romance. During the day she carves out writing time in between trips to the back door as doorman to her four-legged furry child. At night after spending quality time with her husband she chips away at her never-ending TBR pile.

Keep up with Hoosiergirl Publishing here:
https://hoosiergirl-publishing.kit.com/df28902ff9

You can find all her links on her website:
https://www.laremenicky.com

Also from the Lavish Publishing family

SAMANTHA JACOBEY

Rendered (Irrevocable Series Book 1)
Samantha Jacobey
https://books2read.com/Rendered

The end of the world is coming, or so they say, and that puts Bailey Dewitt on a crash course with Armageddon. Orphaned, she and her young brothers find themselves living with their renegade uncle as part of a group of survivalists. She struggles against them, searching for a way to escape, but every discovery only terrifies her more.

For Caleb Cross, the Ranch is a way of life. The members of their group are family, and none should come between them. Smitten from the moment he met Bailey, his choices are no longer easy, his path no longer clear. He wants to welcome her and the twins into their fold and hopes his kin will agree.

But the elders who lead them aren't interested in the troublesome girl. They are plotting for the time they will be rid of her and expect Caleb to go along with their plans - he is after all one of them.

At first, Bailey resists Caleb's charms, but soon must admit that she desperately needs a friend. She has no intention of anything more, but when the elders make their move, she is forced to trust him with her very life.

They both have hard lessons to learn. Relationships built on secrets and lies don't come with guarantees. When the world falls apart around them, some things are Irrevocable.

Realistic sci-fi and romantic suspense will pull you into to the first book of the Irrevocable Trilogy.

Summer's Deceit (The Trilogy Book 1)
Sara J. Bernhardt
https://books2read.com/SummersDeceit

Jane Callahan is a reclusive, seventeen-year-old high school student dealing with the death of her beloved brother. Her home in Southern California with her mother is a constant reminder of her loss and pain. In hopes of escaping her past she moves to North Bend Oregon to live with her father, where she meets a beautiful boy named Aidan Summers.

Jane is intrigued by his looks as well as his unusual ways of attempting to get her attention. After months of uncommon conversation and frustration, an uncertain romance brews between Jane and Aidan, but Aidan has a ghastly secret that could destroy everything.

Get swept away by The Hunter's Trilogy – YA romantic suspense with a paranormal twist.